BEYOND THE SWIRL

Enjoy the adventure!
Lester Blum

Lester Blum

Illustrated by Chi Fung Wong

The imaginative mind allows one "to raise new questions, new possibilities, to regard old problems from a new angle…"
—Albert Einstein

Man is only limited by the scope of his imagination. *Beyond the Swirl* was written to stimulate the imagination.

This story is dedicated to my grand-nephews: Joshua Samuel Scott, Bryson Yuma Hamada-Scott, and Hunter Rahmy Scott as they travel in life being inquisitive, adventurous, and imaginative. The world is open before them to explore in order to make their mark upon it.

Introduction

It was the hot, humid summer of 1953. We were traveling in our family's brand new two-door Chevrolet coup from Corpus Christi, Texas to New York City. It was an ambitious journey for a new driver with two children under the age of 6 to travel in the sweltering summer heat in a non-air-conditioned car.

Since my mother did not know how to drive, we had a co-driver for most of the trip - a sailor who was on leave who wanted to get to Ohio to visit his family.

There is very little I remember about the trip other than the hot wind blowing through the windows and the large maps that everyone was constantly trying to refold in the wind. The days seemed to go on forever. By the time we got near Ohio to drop off the sailor, I became ill, with a fever. I remained so for the duration of the trip.

I vividly remember driving through the long, bleak Holland Tunnel wondering if it would collapse with us still driving through. We were in New York, but, we kept driving for what seemed like hours. Finally we arrived at my grandparents' apartment building on Hoe Avenue in the Bronx. A comedy worthy of an *I Love Lucy* episode ensued. My father could not parallel park and there was my grandfather, who had no clue I might add, giving him instructions which seemed to be backwards. Finally, after struggling with the car for at least a half an hour, we were parked.

My Aunt Idie and Uncle Lee also lived in the same building, so, between the two apartments, there was room for all of us. I stayed with my grandparents so my Bubbie, Grandmother, could take care of me as she had before when we lived in New York. Several times during our visit, a doctor came to the apartment to give me, what I now believe to be, sulfa injections for my infection. I only recall going out of the apartment occasionally to visit relatives. Not much excitement for a six year old.

An adventure was being planned by Aunt Idie and Uncle Lee to the Museum of Natural History for my younger cousin and me. I was determined that I would feel well enough to go. That morning I got dressed, ate a bowl of oatmeal, which was not my favorite breakfast food, and announced that I was feeling fine. Since the fever seemed to be down, my mother agreed to let me go on the adventure.

And what an adventure it was! I was in awe of everything we saw in the museum, but the dinosaurs held a special fascination. I was frightened yet amazed by the mere size of the bones and their teeth. I did not want to leave the dinosaur section of the museum.

Reluctantly, I agreed to leave when told that we were going to the Gift Shop to find each of us a souvenir. Once in the shop, I let go of Uncle Lee's hand as I headed directly to the Dinosaur display. There I found a small metal baby Pterodactyl – a flying Pterosaur. While Aunt Idie was purchasing the mini statue, Uncle Lee found a picture book about dinosaurs which he bought for me. For years I cherished both the book which I read until it was falling apart and my Pterodactyl who I named Leicester.

My Pterodactyl has been with me for over six decades. Perhaps, subconsciously, he sparked the following story, *Beyond the Swirl.*

Prologue

Before recorded time, the world was dominated by titans. These behemoths, who were later known as Dinosaurs, ruled the world for millions of years. Most early dinosaurs were small bipeds. As they evolved, they adapted to the changing land mass and environment. Some species grew to gigantic proportions. By the height of their reign, the reptiles dominated the land, sea, and sky.

The basic traits and behaviors of dinosaurs were no different than those of today's creatures which includes man. While some were herbivores (plant eaters), others were carnivores (meat eaters), and still others were omnivores (ate both plants and meat); they developed attributes and skills to protect themselves in order to survive in their environment.

After a reign of 200 million years, a catastrophic global event took place about 65 million years ago which caused the mass extinction of the dinosaurs. The demise of the dinosaurs is still unexplained. There are many theories as to the cause of the mass extinction. Whether it was a meteorite or comet that hit the earth or massive volcanic eruptions or global flooding which changed the sea levels, the end result was the same. The Age of the Dinosaur had ended but, their descendants, the birds, are still among us today.

The day began as many others, but, this one held the promise of an adventure that no one could ever imagine.

Alex awoke extremely early with warm sunlight streaming across his face. His alarm clock has always been the New York City sounds of honking cars, trucks, and sirens which filtered through his closed windows. The sounds and his feeling of anticipation caused him to become fully awake. Anxious for the day to begin, he jumped out of bed. Today was the day that he and Cathy, his younger sister, were going on a Day Camp excursion to the Natural History Museum. This was a great break from the games, swimming, and arts and crafts that they had been doing all summer. Day Camp seemed like punishment for not being in school rather than the fun advertised. Alex was primed for the adventure.

While brushing his teeth, he could hear Cathy screaming for their mother to help her dress. Was his excitement contagious or maybe she was genuinely excited about the day's prospects as well. It is hard to understand exactly how a five year old's mind works. That is not to say that you can understand an eight year old's any better.

Almost simultaneously the two of them ran like a stampeding herd of buffalo into the large kitchen.

"Stop running, calm down and sit at the table like humans to eat your breakfast" said their Mother.

"Like humans, what did she think we were?" thought Alex.

Breakfast was a treat for a weekday morning with pancakes, turkey bacon, and his favorite – wild Maine blueberry syrup. Of course there were the required glasses of orange juice for Alex and apple juice for

Cathy. They both also had the dreaded glass of milk sitting in front of them. Cathy was allergic to almost everything, so her milk was vanilla flavored Soy Milk. "Why can't I have the soy milk? It tastes much better than this old cow juice." Alex made this comment every morning except today.

"Are you feeling OK, Alex? You woke up extremely early, even washed your glasses and have not said a word about your sister's milk" asked his Mother.

"Yes, I'm fine. Just want to get going! The sooner we get there the more we can do" answered Alex.

"Well, just remember to stay with your group, listen to the group leaders, and keep a watchful eye on your sister. You know she is only in the camp because you are there to watch over her." Actually, his mother did not need to play the guilt card as Alex always wanted to take care of Cathy. She was his confidant, best friend, and playmate.

His mother must have had the foresight of an old gypsy fortune teller as her worries were yet to unfold. But, we are getting ahead of ourselves.

Alex ate his breakfast with the speed of a voracious lion. He grabbed his dishes and literally threw them into the sink much to his mother's dismay. He ran to his room to get out of his pajamas and finish getting ready. He pulled a pair of shorts and socks out of his drawer and scurried into the living room to find a camp shirt in the bag of clean laundry his father had picked up on the way home last night. Alex opened the bag, dumped the contents on the sofa and searched to find the obnoxious neon orange Do More Summer Day Camp T shirt that everyone had to wear. The same color every day, five days a week. No wonder he had headaches when he came home from camp.

The essentials – wallet with an identification card, Metro Card, emergency ten dollars and the old Boy Scout compass Uncle Stefan had given him last summer when they were exploring Central Park – were put into his pockets.

Belt on and backpack in hand, Alex returned to the kitchen to hurry Cathy along and, of course, his mother since she had to take them to the day camp. "I don't know why I can't take Cathy myself. I am a big boy and know the way. I can do it" whined Alex in his attempt to speed everyone up.

"Give yourself a few years. It is too dangerous now for you to travel by yourself."

"I won't be by myself; Cathy will be with me."

"I give up! I have to brush Cathy's hair which you know gets all tangled because it is very curly. So it will take a while to get her ready. I'll be right back as soon as we finish and we will go. Watch some cartoons or something" said his Mother.

It seemed like an eternity, but they were finally ready. Lunches were packed into backpacks, shoes tied, and permission slips signed. Off to day camp…

More waiting! It took the elevator a lifetime to open the doors on their floor. At last they reached the lobby. The front door was in sight. Out into the sweltering heat of the New York summer they went, hand in hand to walk over to the subway station on 86th Street.

It was still early in the morning yet the heat was bearing down upon them and the sidewalk's retained heat was emanating up. They were being bombarded from top and bottom.

"I'm melting" whined Cathy.

"We all are" responded their Mother. "Let's go to the subway."

Cathy took off her backpack and pulled out a large red fan. After whipping it open, she began fanning herself like a true "Princess". Where she got that from was beyond anyone's comprehension. "I'm ready to walk now."

As they walked to Broadway, Alex let his imagination wander since he had walked that route so many times, he could do it blindfolded. The tall apartment buildings in the upper Westside were like the walls of a canyon – steep and high. They were walking in the urban valley towards the subterranean train – The Subway. The camp was on 14th Street which seemed to be alien territory to Alex. Downtown there was a mix of businesses and apartment buildings – Wall Street to the Freedom Tower and the Staten Island Ferry from which you could see the Statue of Liberty.

Alex and Cathy had to travel from uptown on the Westside to the camp on 14th Street and yet, the Museum was again uptown. So, they had to travel downtown to turn around in an hour or so to go back uptown to almost where they lived. None of this made sense to Alex. "Why are grown-ups so stupid?" he wondered. All this extra traveling was limiting his time at the museum.

Arriving at Camp, the goodbye kisses were given. Alex cringed and wiped his cheek with his hand.

"Mom, must you do this in public - in front of my friends? It is embarrassing. I am not a kid."

Alex turned quickly towards the entrance. Cathy and he entered through the automated handicap door to find their respective Camp counselors – Todd and Shanisha. The campers were running around the lobby playing chase, screaming, laughing – completely out of control.

One more hour before they would leave for the museum. The minutes were not clicking away fast enough. This was torture!

Finally, the time arrived. Suddenly they heard Todd shouting over the mayhem, "line up against the wall so we can go to the Museum."

Alex thought, "How does lining up against a wall make you go to the Museum? It did not make sense."

The counselors found it difficult to control and organize the kids when they were so wild and excited about their adventure for the day. And they thought being a counselor would be an easy summer job. This was nothing like what they expected.

They each raised their voice to call roll of their respective groups. This merely added to the already deafening volume.

"Kent Abbott"

"Yes"

"Jose Sanchez"

"Aquí"

"Sally Chan"

"What?"

"Thomas Foley"

"Present and accounted for"

"Thea Brown"

"I'm here, you know that"

"Alex Stein"

Complete silence.

"ALEX STEIN"

Alex was lost in his own world not paying attention to this nonsense until Jose kicked his leg. "What? Oh, here"

Todd continued with the roll call but was clearly annoyed by the lack of attention he was getting. "Listen guys – if you want to have a good day at the Museum, you better get with the program. Shanisha and I are not going to put up with any nonsense or anyone not listening or not staying together."

More delays! Now Shanisha asked for everyone's permission slip. Alex put his hands on the side of his head shaking it in disbelief. He was thinking that this could have been done an hour ago when they checked in. But NO – they had to do it now.

Finally, after checking the permission slips, Shanisha announced that they were ready to go.

"Listen up. We are going to walk to the subway and ride uptown to the Museum. At the 79th Street stop we will walk over to the Museum so it is important for you to remember who your buddy is and always hold his hand", announced Todd.

"But what if your buddy is a girl? You said to hold *his* hand", asked the group's resident genius, Thomas.

"Very funny! It is a figure of speech. You hold your buddy's hand whether the buddy is a boy or girl. Got it? Or do you want to stay here?"

So off they went to catch the Number 1 train walking alongside the buildings to avoid the heat of the glaring sun - two by two holding hands very much like Noah's ark. They went down the subway steps and through the turnstile still holding hands for fear of being reprimanded by Todd or Shanisha.

It felt like they had left the oven created by the sun to enter into the fiery mouth of the dragon. They were suffocating waiting on the platform for the Number 1 train. After waiting a very long twelve minutes, the Number 1 train which was headed towards 242nd Street arrived.

Boarding the train and the ride itself was filled with turmoil. "Are they all here?" Todd and Shanisha questioned themselves nervously. They were afraid that they might lose someone in the confusion. Bedlam had begun which was not unusual whenever a group of kids were together. There was a scrambling for seats. This was followed by the shifting around so this one could sit with that one and that one with this one. "Move over to make room so others can sit." "No you cannot swing on the pole." The decibel level was deafening. "Lower your voices." "Do not eat your snacks now." "Stay away from the doors – people have to get in and out of the train." The ride was total chaos.

Alex chose to ignore all that was going on around him telling anyone who would listen about the wonders they would be seeing at the Museum. After all, he was an EXPERT having been there with Uncle Stefan a few months ago to see the special frog exhibit. Alex could hardly contain his excitement. He kept fidgeting in his seat, turning to this one and then that one, jumping up to talk to those swinging around the pole.

But, no one was really interested in anything Alex had to tell them. Even Cathy was preoccupied with the ride itself and the shenanigans of her fellow campers.

"Sit down now. Alex. You're going to fall when the train stops", shouted Todd. It was obvious that the passengers were disturbed, annoyed, and angry with the antics of this unruly bunch of kids.

"Ok", in an extremely loud voice, "ok everyone. Listen up. We are getting off at the next stop. Get ready, make sure you have everything. Take your buddy's hand. When you get off the train, go directly to the back wall of the platform and line up single file." Todd gave so many instructions, the group of 5 to 10 year olds got confused. Of course Thomas had a thing or two to say, while laughing hysterically, "How can we line up single file if we are holding our buddy's hand?" Thomas thought it was funny to use his clever mind to act like the comedian of the group.

Todd's response was far from acceptable. "No time to explain, we have to get off NOW. Just do what I say."

So there they were on the 79th Street platform in some sort of jagged single file line in a bizarre configuration because they were holding their buddy's hand. Interestingly they all marched to the end of the platform and up the stairs silently. Perhaps they were frightened of Todd or what they anticipated seeing in the Museum.

This fear dissipated immediately once they were on the street at Broadway and 79th Street in front of a large church. Silence was broken, hands released and mayhem ensued, once again.

The corner was crowded with people at the newsstand, others waiting to cross the street, and a congregation of homeless people sitting or lying on the steps of the church. Todd and Shanisha had to re-establish control over this rebel body, otherwise, they would never make it to the museum.

Lined up once again, two by two, holding hands with their buddy, the orange fledglings commenced their march across Broadway and east on 79th Street towards the museum. At Columbus Avenue they were facing the back of the Museum.

The back of the building was large and imposing like the place where the evil guy in a horror movie would live. Shadowing the sidewalk was a canopy of large trees. Hearing an unusual amount of cackling and chirping, Alex looked up into the high branches to see hundreds of black birds –crows – looking down on him. Alex was fascinated with the mysterious birds, the building, and the awaiting adventure.

Todd and Shanisha were not sure where to go to enter the Museum. They looked at the map the camp activities director had given them. They decided that the group should walk on 77th Street and enter through the main entrance on Central Park West. Of course it would have been easier for everyone to enter through the West Pavilion off of Columbus or even on 81st into the Grand Foyer. But no, they unnecessarily marched the youngsters around the entire Museum.

By the time they arrived at the main entrance, they were exhausted from the walking and the heat. Everyone had to sit down on the steps of the museum to rest for a few minutes. Alex was annoyed, he was anxious to get inside and explore. "Todd, let's go. They will close before we see everything." The group started to get rowdy which Shanisha assumed to mean they were rested, so she suggested that they go inside.

As they entered the museum, the fossilized bones of a Barosaurus, a gigantic 90 foot long herbivore, was directly in front of them. The Barosaurus was displayed rearing up to protect its young from an attacking Allosaurus. The Allosaurus was a two-ton killing machine. Even as just bones, this Allosaurus looked menacing with huge yellowed razor-sharp teeth and curved claws designed to rip open the throat of its prey. Everyone was both fascinated and frightened by the sight of those huge skeletons appearing to fight each other.

Alex was frozen in awe at the sight. It was almost as if HE had become an exhibit. When his friend Jose's attempts to bring him back to reality failed, Cathy tugged at his shirt and he came out of his trance. "What is it, Alex?" asked Cathy. Alex was dumbfounded; "a dinosaur who lived a long time ago" was all he could answer.

"But, he is just a bunch of bones, like what is left when we eat steak" according to Cathy.

Alex chose to ignore Cathy's comment and as the two of them moved forward with the neon orange brigade towards the School Group Check In desk, Alex kept looking back mesmerized by the mere size of the Barosaurus. The bones were conjuring up images of another world for him and Cathy to explore.

Once at the desk, Shanisha lined the children up against the wall again while Todd signed the group in. Alex felt that all this lining up and waiting was a pure waste of time. They would have already been inside exploring had they come with their parents or Uncle Stefan. There was so much he wanted to see and also show to Cathy who had never been to a museum before. His time is valuable and they were limiting it.

At last they started towards the staircase to go to the second floor. Someone had decided that they should see the African mammal exhibit first. Alex told Cathy, "It's a waste of time to see stuffed animals when we've seen real ones at the zoo, watched baby monkeys play and even rode an elephant." Oh well, they had no choice. Maybe today was not going to offer the excitement Alex had anticipated.

The museum curators tried to make the mammal exhibits look like pictures Alex had seen of Africa. The nature programs his father watched were far more interesting. He was not impressed.

"Alex, I have to pee", Cathy whined while standing pushing her knees together as if trying to hold it.

"Ok, Ok, Cathy, I'll take you to the little girl's room. I saw one by the stairs as we came up. You can go on your own, right?"

"Of course, I'm not a baby."

"No, of course not. Let's go. Don't forget to flush and wash your hands." Alex was beginning to sound like his mother – scary!

When Cathy finally came out of the bathroom, her hands were dripping water. "I couldn't reach the paper towels." Alex dried her hands on his T shirt. They slowly worked their way back to the African mammal exhibit stopping along the way to explore whatever there was to be seen, which wasn't much in his opinion.

Entering the hall, they saw that it was empty except for a few old people. Todd, Shanisha, Thomas, Jose, and all the rest of the Day Campers were gone.

Alex was in shock and nervous for a brief moment. "Don't worry, we'll find them, Cathy. While we look for the rest of the kids, we can explore things that WE want to see." Of course, Cathy agreed as she had full faith and trust in her older brother's abilities.

Taking Cathy's hand, they approached a security guard standing in the doorway of the exhibit guarding the stuffed animals. Really, what was there to guard? "Where are the dinosaurs? I forgot on which floor our Mother told us to meet her."

The guard looked at them closely. The young boy seemed confident and assured, but little girl looked to be perplexed and confused.

"You will find them on the fourth floor. But, are you sure you will be ok? You both seem very young for your mother to leave you alone to find your own way."

Alex placed his hands on his hips and in a positive voice said, "Oh yes, we do this all the time in museums."

"Strange to me, but, that's the modern way of encouraging independence, I guess. Take the stairs at the end of the hall – on the left outside this door" the guard said as he pointed in that direction.

It was not an easy climb for Cathy. It was a lot of steps for a young child to climb from the second to the fourth floors and Alex was patient as he usually was. At last they arrived. In front of them was the Hall of the Saurischian Dinosaurs – the current realm of the dinosaurs.

"It's all bones" Cathy complained. Cathy was disappointed. She started in with her whining, "Where are the dinosaurs? I want to play with the little ones like in the zoo in Central Park." In an angry tone, "Who wants to see bones? This is not fun!" She sat down on the floor – pouting.

Alex was at a loss for he, too, was disappointed. He had been expecting more than skeletons. What exactly he wasn't sure but definitely more than old bones. Hoping that Cathy would not have another tantrum, he suggested as a way of encouraging her, "Let's look around. Maybe they have them in cages somewhere."

Cathy immediately perked up. "Ok" Cathy said making a game out of the search. "I'll go this way and you go that way." She had no idea of what was awaiting them.

Off they went in opposite directions to scout the hall for "live" dinosaurs and hopefully some "little ones" for Cathy to play with as if that was really going to happen, but, they were hopeful.

While looking at the bones in one of the display cases, Alex sensed that the light was fading. It was more than just a visual dimming of the light – he felt it. Darkness was encompassing him. A large blackened shadow seemed to pass above his head totally obscuring the room lights.

Suddenly he heard a loud terrified scream. When he heard it again, Alex realized that it was Cathy who was screaming. It was not a normal scream like when their mother pulled her curly ginger hair while brushing it, but, a blood curdling scream that was terrifying. As he ran around the corner of the display towards the screams of terror, he saw an extremely large black bird, which looked like a giant crow, flying in a circle with its neck craned towards the floor spotting its prey. Suddenly, in a flash of black feathers, the bird swooped down and grabbed Cathy with its talons. "Alex, Help Me!" screamed Cathy. Still clenching Cathy, the bird flapped his enormous wings which created a violent wind current while soaring to the ceiling of the exhibit hall. They flew around the room faster and faster. Alex was helpless. Without any other idea, he rushed to open his backpack to see if he could come up with something. In an act of desperation, he threw his apple and sandwich at the bird thinking that if the bird had something else to eat, he would drop Cathy. Falling to the ground seemed a better choice for Cathy than being carried around in the air to what purpose by this creature. It was all to no avail. The offering was ignored. The apple and sandwich fell to the ground. The bird held on to Cathy by the straps of her back pack with his claws.

While Alex was looking for additional weapons, the bird abruptly flew lower flapping his wings with such violence that feathers were falling out filling the air with large black plumes. Its speed seemed to increase as if it were an airplane on the runway getting ready to take off. The bird was on a collision course with a large vertical glass display case. Alex rushed after them. The bird did not hesitate on his collision course. He did not crash into the glass. He literally flew through the glass which now appeared like a translucent, shimmery,

swirling, glutinous mass of clear jello. They were in the display case. Alex could not see them anymore. Where were they? The glass solidified and became transparent again. They were not visible in the case.

Alex approached the case and gently put his hands on the glass. He ran his hands as high and as wide as he could reach. It was solid glass. Inside were the bones of a dinosaur called Deinonychus. He was small for a dinosaur, being only about eleven feet long with a hooked claw on his hind feet. Reading the description, Alex figured out that this dinosaur was similar to early birds. But what was the connection and where was Cathy; why did the giant bird take her?

What was he going to do? Alex was totally distraught. Cathy was his responsibility!

Alex examined the case from the top as far as he could reach all the way to the wooden base. Not finding any way to get into the case and without any hesitation, Alex decided that if the bird and Cathy could go through the glass, then so could he. He backed away from the case going down the aisle between the cases to give himself enough distance for a running start. As he pulled on his back pack, he launched into his fastest playground run, full speed straight towards the case. Scared beyond belief and anticipating crashing into the glass, Alex covered his eyes as best he could with his arms and kept running.

The impact was like squishing jello through the spaces between his teeth. Suddenly Alex was inside, but, where was he? He recovered from his state of shock when he heard Cathy's voice as if in an echo chamber, "Alex, come see this." When he opened his eyes, everything seemed hazy, out of focus, so unreal! He thought maybe his glasses were dirty, so he took them off and wiped them on his shirt. When he put them back on his vision started to clear up. He saw Cathy sitting on a large, flat rock with the huge black bird perched by her side. The scene was unreal – a different dimension. It was almost as if the black bird was watching over Cathy. Suddenly, without any warning, the bird launched into flight straight up into the bright sky. Higher and higher he went until he totally disappeared.

As he looked around, all Alex could see were large rocks and a dry, parched land. The air was hot and stifling like when they were in the desert near Las Vegas last year. It burned his nostrils just to breathe. Plant life was extremely sparse. The only things that seemed to be growing in this earth and heat were giant ferns and conifers – with long pointed needles and huge pine cones very much like large Christmas trees.

This was definitely a strange land. If they were not in New York as was obvious – where were they?

"Alex, look what I found. You have to come see this", Cathy's insistence snapped Alex out of his thoughts. He walked over to where Cathy was squatting.

"It's a nest. And it is full of eggs, Alex, and look, this one is moving." Cathy was fascinated by the massive bundle of twigs huddled against the rocks with the smooth large orbs hidden within. Alex was already getting more nervous with each passing moment. These eggs were huge, bigger than even the ostrich egg Uncle Stefan had on display on the bookshelf in his living room. Whoever or whatever laid these eggs had to be around nearby which meant it would be dangerous for them to stick around.

The moving egg began to crack. A slimy reptilian creature making croaking noises began to emerge from the cracked shell. As it crawled out, a sharp snapping sound was heard as the shell fell away from the reptile.

Almost simultaneously Alex felt the ground vibrate. Around the left side of the rock, a gigantic head appeared.

"No way, Cathy. That is a baby Plateosaurus and that monstrosity is its Mother. Run!"

Cathy couldn't move. The twenty-nine-foot-long Plateosaurus was blocking her way. After nuzzling the baby to clear off the slime and help it get completely out of the shell, the Plateosaurus turned her attention to Cathy.

Cathy was frozen with fright. She was as still as a statue, neither able to cry nor move. The Plateosaurus was equally stunned by this strange looking and smelling creature. She leaned forward; picked Cathy up in her mouth before placing her gently alongside the nest.

Cathy wiped the thick smelly saliva off her face and arms. "Gross!"

Alex began jumping up and down, waving his arms and shouting, "Over here! Over here! Come get me! Come on", in an effort to distract the Plateosaurus from Cathy.

The Plateosaurus displayed little interest in any of Alex's antics. She was more concerned with her hatchlings. More of them were beginning to come out of their shells. Cathy was no longer scared. She was fascinated, watching each egg crack open and seeing new life emerge. Without thinking about it, she even

picked up one of the babies, wiping it with her T shirt. At that point, the mother Plateosaurus stomped her huge foot right next to Cathy, shaking the ground, demonstrating her disapproval.

Cathy returned the baby to the nest with the rest of his siblings. She was mesmerized by these creatures. "Alex, are we in the cage with the dinosaurs?"

"I don't think so. This seems too real - very weird," answered Alex.

The mother was being protective of not only her babies, but also of Cathy. Alex tried to figure out a way to get closer. The Plateosaurus was aware of each attempt Alex made. She would rear up into a bipedal position, reaching out to expose a large clawed thumb. This posturing by the monster deterred Alex from any further rescue attempts - for now.

He had a brilliant idea. He opened his back pack to see if he had anything he could use to distract the mother. He found a health bar and decided something sweet might do the trick. Maybe she would react well. Besides, he did not like the flavor of that bar and Cathy couldn't eat it because, of course, she was allergic to peanuts.

Alex crawled forward very slowly as he had seen in war movies and left the unwrapped health bar on the ground before returning to his safe area. The Plateosaurus inched forward sniffing towards the bar. Her breathing was so intense that the dirt on the ground began flying around like a dust storm causing Cathy to start sneezing. The Plateosaurus lifted her head for a brief moment before returning to her sniffing quest. Finally, her flared nostrils reached the bar. She smelled it for a moment, moved it with her muzzle, and quickly devoured it in one bite. It certainly wasn't her normal vegetation diet.

The bribe did the trick. Alex could slowly come forward and sit beside Cathy. He gave her some wet wipes from his backpack to blow her nose and to wipe off the slime and grime.

Whether it was the heat, the strain of what they had been experiencing or a combination of both, they were collapsing with exhaustion.

"I don't know what we are going to do, but, I can't even think. We need to rest. We'll figure this all out later." Cathy, who was struggling to keep her eyes open, leaned against him and was asleep immediately.

They must have slept several hours under the watchful eye of the Plateosaurus with her babies scampering over the rocks and them. They were so exhausted that even the babies using them as a playground did not wake them.

Diffused voices caused Alex to wake from his deep slumber. The voices were muffled and barely understandable. They reminded him of when his mother would speak to him while he was swimming underwater.

"Alex! Cathy!"

Hearing their names brought Alex to a state of being fully awake. The voices were Todd and Shanisha. But, where were they?

Alex whispered back, so as not to wake Cathy, "Here! We are HERE!"

The Day Campers had just completed their visit to the Hall of African peoples. Shanisha gathered the group. She escorted them into the hallway of Birds of the World.

"Line up with your buddy over by the stairs", Shanisha instructed. "We are going to climb the stairs, as a group, to the next floor to see the American Indian exhibits. There is a bathroom right upstairs if anyone has to go."

As Shanisha looked down the line-up, she saw that one boy and one girl did not have a buddy. "Thomas, Thea where are your buddies?"

Thomas shrugged his shoulders. "I have no clue."

"I don't know", responded Thea.

Shanisha looked around, not seeing either Alex or Cathy. She stepped back into the Hall of African Peoples. "Todd, do you see Alex and Cathy? They are not out in the hall yet."

"No, I'll look around."

A few moments later, Todd responded that they were not in the gallery.

Reality sank in. "Todd, we have a major problem. We've lost two campers! They're LOST!"

"Alex! Cathy!" Shanisha and Todd called out.

In the meantime, without the supervision of their counselors, the campers began running around the hallway, jumping up and down the stairs – uncontrollable. Shanisha spun around and screamed, "Let's get it together. Line up with your buddy. We're going up to the third floor – QUIETLY!"

The group, seeing that Shanisha was agitated, began to climb the stairs as quietly as mice. At the base of the stairs, Todd whispered, with panic in his voice, "Where could they have gone? What are we going to do? We have to find them!"

Shanisha calmly took charge of the search for the missing children. "You go upstairs with the rest of the kids, Todd and I'll enlist the help of the museum security staff to search for them. They couldn't have gone far. I am sure we will find the two of them together."

With a defeated attitude for having "lost" two campers, Todd followed the kids upstairs. Shanisha took the same staircase down; taking two steps at a time in her haste. She headed back to the First Floor to report the missing children to the School Group Check-In desk. Perhaps they could help organize a search.

"Cathy, Alex – where are you?"

The garbled voices gradually faded to complete silence. Alex wasn't sure if he had been dreaming or not. What he did know was that Cathy and he were still alone in this strange land.

He fell back into a deep sleep.

A low, steady grinding growl woke both of them with a start. Alex turned around to see where the menacing sound was coming from. He saw a creature was approaching rapidly across the parched rocky terrain. This sixteen-and-a-half-foot animal had to be a Liliensternus. His blade-like teeth were glistening with saliva. It must be after one of the baby Plateosaurus (and would not reject Alex or Cathy either) as the mother was grazing in a patch of vegetation a short distance away.

While throwing rocks to keep the dinosaur at bay, Alex started screaming what he thought were "war cries". After a near panic attack, Cathy huddled behind him. Between her screams of terror, she began to gather more rocks for Alex to use as ammunition. Each time Alex was able to hit his target with a rock, the Liliensternus roared in anger and lurched forward baring his sharp teeth.

It was like when they played "nerf darts" against Uncle Stefan with Alex doing the shooting and Cathy gathering the spent darts to reuse. Only this time, it was all too real!

"He's going to eat us!" screamed Cathy.

"Yeah, I got that, so get me more rocks!"

The mother Plateosaurus heard the commotion. She lifted her head letting out a bellow of distress that sounded like a fog horn. She started stampeding directly at the Liliensternus. She reared up to her full height to intimidate the predator and also so she could use her clawed thumb to take a powerful swipe at the meat eater.

The thumb grazed the predator's shoulder raising a roar of agony, but not before he bit into the Plateosaurus' belly. When the Liliensternus pulled away, Alex not only saw a gapping raw wound on its shoulder but also dark red blood slowly dripping from his sharp teeth.

It was a good thing Alex played left field in baseball because he learned to throw a ball accurately. One of Alex's rocks connected to the fin crest along the Liliensternus' snout. The dinosaur yelped in pain, once again and then gave up the fight. He fled to nurse his wounds as the Plateosaurus, blood pouring from her belly wound, lumbered after him to make sure he was gone.

The Plateosaurus limped back to the nest area. It was obvious that she was in terrible pain from her wound. She collapsed to the ground with a thunderous thud. She allowed Alex to approach almost with a thankful attitude for helping to save her babies. "Cathy, she is bleeding a lot. Get my swim towel out of my backpack." She brought him the towel which he folded and pressed against the Plateosaurus' belly to help stop the bleeding. He had seen that done on TV. The ground beneath the Plateosaurus was soggy with blood.

After what seemed like an eternity, the Pleateosaurus began to stand up. The towel fell away; the bleeding had mostly stopped. It was a raw open wound with just a little blood still oozing out. She stretched her long neck and licked the wound much like a dog or cat would have done.

She then reared up, stretching upward and pulled down some conifer branches. While she began chewing on one, she pushed another towards Alex and Cathy as a gift as if to say, "Thank You".

They couldn't imagine eating a conifer branch so Cathy broke it up into tiny pieces and fed them to the babies. It surprised both of them that they, being newborn, were able to chew the needles off the stems.

"We have to get out of here. Uncle Stefan always told me, when in doubt, go north and you'll always find your way." Alex took Uncle Stefan's old compass out of his pocket. He placed it on a flat rock so it would be steady. He waited for the magnetic arrow to get its bearings.

The arrow began to swirl completely out of control like it was possessed by a spirit; slowly at first, gaining momentum until it was spinning faster and faster than the eye could follow. Abruptly it stopped. Suddenly the world began to spin. Everything was moving fast. Alex grabbed Cathy and held her tightly.

Everything around the compass, except the ground they were standing on, began to spin out of control. Shapes, colors, sounds were all blurred and muted.

Maybe this is what Uncle Stefan meant when he said, "this compass is like no other. It will lead you to worlds beyond your imagination."

As quickly as it begun, it abruptly stopped. Alex turned his head from side to side, up and down. The entire world was different; everything had changed. Alex could almost hear his heart pounding in his chest. Both he and Cathy were sweating profusely. Alex heard a loud cackle sound and saw the shadows of vast black wings soaring even higher into the cloudless, vibrant violet sky.

Even the air seemed different. It felt more temperate with a higher degree of humidity. They were standing in the center of a vast open prairie amid a herd of huge creatures. Alex was confused again which seemed to be his constant state of affairs.

"Cathy, I don't know where we are or how we got here, but, I do know we are surrounded by Brachiosaurus. I saw a drawing of them in the nature magazine we have at school. These plant eaters are about 85 feet long which is longer than the swimming pool at camp and must weigh a bunch of tons. We have to be careful again."

The mere size and weight of the Brachiosaurus made them a danger to Alex and Cathy.

In the distance you could see that the prairie was surrounded by a lush forest of conifer trees. The herd was lumbering in that direction. The forest offered plenty of food and judging by the density of the plants – water for the Brachiosaurus feeding machines.

They weren't home and this "world" was completely different from the previous one. Without hesitation, Alex began running with Cathy in tow. They darted in and out between the tree trunk size legs of the Brachiosaurus. Alex was trying to get them to the shelter of the forest instead of leaving them exposed on the vast open plain to what new unknown danger!

"Look Alex, a little one," Cathy exclaimed as she ran towards a juvenile Brachiosaurus. The youngster stopped, cocked his head to stare at the strange creatures entering his world. Cathy got closer. She timidly reached out her hand to the lowered head. She actually touched it. His skin felt rough and very dry. The Brachiosaurus seemed as intrigued as she was. He did not move and allowed Cathy to stroke him.

This action drew the attention of an adult, who was apparently the mother, to the existence of Alex and Cathy as well as prompting her ire. The Brachiosaurus, who looked to Alex to be as big as a ten-story building, came stomping at an unbelievable pace across the prairie towards them. In her wake there was a dust storm which obscured everything. They could only see directly in front of them.

"Cathy, leave the baby alone. That big one is charging us to protect him." It was too late. The Brachiosaurus was upon them. With one fell swoop she used her long neck to thrust her head forward connecting with Cathy which sent her flying through the air away from the juvenile. You could hear a bed of conifer branches snap as she landed with a soft thud several feet away from where they had been standing.

"Are you OK?" Alex yelled, as he ran towards her. Cathy was crying hysterically. Being projected into the air frightened her more than anything else. The flight and landing did not hurt her other than some potential bumps which might lead to some colorful bruises.

"Cathy, stop crying. You're fine. It was not even as scary as the roller coaster ride in Coney Island." As quickly as the tear faucet was turned on, it shut off. Cathy was just stunned.

In the meantime, the juvenile Brachiosaurus rushed in an uncoordinated gait from the opposite direction to where Cathy was lying on the ground. He reached Cathy before Alex did and began licking her tears, legs, and arms in a playful, friendly manner. "Yuck, he's slobbering all over me. He has doggie breath. Gross!" When Alex bent down to check her for any cuts and bruises, the Brachiosaurus used his weight to push him away as if HE were protecting Cathy.

As the attacking mother gradually approached, she lowered her head to sniff Alex as she passed him. When she got to her child and Cathy, she knelt on her front legs like they have seen elephants do in the zoo. First, she nuzzled the juvenile before licking Cathy's face. Was she apologizing to Cathy for knocking her half way across the savannah?

"It's ok, I'm not hurt", Cathy told the mother as she struggled to get up. As if she understood, the mother Brachiosaurus allowed Cathy to take hold of her neck for support as she lifted herself off the ground. Alex went to Cathy unimpeded by the dinosaurs. She was shaken with a purplish bruise beginning to form on her leg, but, otherwise, she was ok. The juvenile rubbed his front shoulder first against Cathy and then, surprisingly, Alex. It appeared as if they were being accepted by both the Brachiosaurus.

Cathy hugged the juvenile as if he were her favorite stuffed animal, Floppy, the rabbit which she carried around constantly at home.

The four of them rejoined the herd. They began walking toward the forest. When Cathy started slowing down, faltering in her steps, the juvenile nudged her along.

Alex knew that they could not keep up the same pace as the herd. He was becoming exhausted, so he could only imagine how Cathy felt even though she was not complaining. And that was a first.

He took a chance – he got in front of Cathy, put his hands under her arms and lifted her up placing her on the back of the juvenile who, after the initial shock, did not seem to mind.

What a scientific discovery! Uncle Stefan would be proud. Cathy was probably the first kid to ever ride a real dinosaur.

They traveled this way for what seemed like hours. Alex began stumbling, holding on to the juvenile's neck for support. Almost sensing an immediate collapse, the mother Brachiosaurus stopped in front of Alex, blocking his way. She laid down on the ground making movements with her neck and head almost summoning him to her. He hobbled towards her when suddenly she hit him with her head knocking him into her upper shoulder area. "I got it", Alex said. "You want me to get on just like Cathy." With a little effort, he straddled her neck. The giant rose to her feet.

"I'm on the top of the world!" he screamed with excitement.

Off they went with the herd. Alex hung on for dear life for if he fell, he thought it would be like dropping from the Empire State Building.

By nightfall they had entered into the dark, damp, mysterious forest. Strange scratching sounds were heard coming from the dense undergrowth. These sounds did not seem to disturb the Brachiosaurus. As the herd began gorging themselves on the smorgasbord of greens, Alex and Cathy slid off the Brachiosaurus. They stumbled towards a large tree away from the grazing animals. They were immediately asleep as they fell against the base of a tree with their new best friend, the juvenile Brachiosaurus, sleeping by their side.

The dawn, as it were, broke with bold flashes of light and the sharp crack of thunder. It started to rain – not just a normal rain, but, a torrential thunderstorm. Alex and Cathy huddled close to the tree trunk for shelter. While the canopy of the forest undulated back and forth from the force of the wind and rain, the tops of the trees were dense enough to act as a large natural umbrella which kept them relatively dry.

The Brachiosaurus were undeterred by the rain storm. They were wandering around the immediate area pulling leaves and small plants to gnaw on for breakfast.

"I'm starving, Alex."

Cathy's comment made Alex realize how hungry he was. He emptied the contents of both his and Cathy's backpacks to see what they had left to eat. Not much – one bottle of water, a full apple juice container, a baggy with pretzel sticks, one apple, and one sliced turkey sandwich with lettuce.

"Cathy, we have very little left to eat. Let's each just split a half of the sandwich for now and save the rest for later. We can drink the water and then I'll fill the empty bottle with the rain water dripping down the tree trunk. Hopefully it will be okay to drink."

"Alright Alex. I am not too hungry anyway. Maybe we should try some of the leaves the Brachio whatever are eating?"

"Yeah, right. If we must. We'll try them later. Watch what leaves and plants they are eating. All these leaves look the same to me. The way our luck is going, we are liable to chew some poison ivy." It was great that Alex could maintain some sense of humor which served to encourage both Cathy and himself.

Suddenly the sky became violent. The wind gained hurricane force which neither of them had ever experienced before. The wind whipped the branches back and forth. Some branches began to snap off the trees falling along with the rain. Thunder bolts of bright lightning flashed through the leaves. They were almost blinded by the intensity of the pure white flashes.

The Brachiosaurus who were becoming visibly agitated, swayed their small heads back and forth with their necks like a jump rope. Alex and Cathy stayed close to their spot by the tree to keep out of everyone's way. Mixed in with the sound of the storm there was a second thunderous sound and then a deafening roar which muted the sound of the thunder.

The trees seemed to part like curtains in the theater. Between the trunks two gigantic dinosaurs emerged walking upright on extremely muscular bird-like legs. They were at least 25 feet tall with three sharp curved clawed fingers at the end of their short arms. But it was their mouths that sent a chill of terror through the clearing – their jaws were lined with at least seventy razor sharp teeth browned probably with the dried blood of their previous meals. These beasts were the dreaded Allosaurus, the most ferocious carnivores living.

The Allosaurus were shrewd hunters. They seemed to understand the importance of cooperation to be successful in the hunt. The larger Allosaurus lurched forward striking out at one of the Brachiosaurus to distract the others in the herd. Other Brachiosaurus ushered the juveniles into the center of a ring. They surrounded them to protect their young and to fight off any attack. The other Allosaurus paced around the circle growling, baring his teeth and striking occasionally with his claws. Finally, he saw his chance. He leaped forward, crashing through the circle, grabbed one of the infants with his clawed hand and put it directly into his crushing jaws.

Seeing that the other Allosaurus was successful, the large one turned his attention to the unfamiliar smell wafting in the air. Following the scent, he saw the two small creatures by the trees. Alex and Cathy were being eyed as an Allosaurus dessert. As quickly as he could, Alex swooped Cathy up, partially carrying, and partially dragging her along the slippery, wet ground towards the circle of adult Brachiosaurus. A tremendous Brachiosaurus male, weighing as much as two elephants, saw the Allosaurus go after the kids. He broke the circle and placed his large bulk between the kids and the carnivore. Alex and Cathy crawled between the barrier of Brachiosaurus bulk into the circle and crouched down by their friend, the juvenile Brachiosaurus.

The second Allosaurus dropped his prey by the trees on the far side to be retrieved later. He joined the first to fight the brave Brachiosaurus. They went in for the kill. An extremely bloody battle took place. While the Brachiosaurus was able to inflict some damage on one of the Allosaurus when he fell on his leg, crushing it by his weight, the Allosaurus were ultimately victorious. With the Brachiosaurus down, the other Allosaurus shredded his throat with his teeth, while the one on the ground ripped open his belly with his claws.

Alex and Cathy huddled even closer to the juvenile. The noise level was deafening. All the dinosaurs were howling in fear. Cathy was screaming. Alex was in shock, but he did manage to cover Cathy's eyes so she would not see any more blood and gore.

The dying Brachiosaurus let out a loud agonizing bellow. There was no time to check on their fallen companion. The herd took this final shriek as a chance to escape. They knew that the Allosaurus would be preoccupied ripping apart the body.

The group rapidly reformed with the juveniles and females to the front guarded by the males in the rear. The mother Brachiosaurus stopped by Alex and Cathy and, once again, made those strange movements with her head which seemed to indicate for them to get on her neck. Without any hesitation, Alex and Cathy wrapped their arms around her neck and pulled themselves up. It was like climbing up on the arc ladder in the playground. They swayed back and forth on their perch, barely managing to stay on in the blinding rain which made the Brachiosaurus' neck very slippery. The herd swiftly left the battle area for the safety of a new section of the forest miles away.

The storm ended. Sunlight broke through the puffy grey clouds. Now this world seemed tranquil. Life was continuing as if nothing at all had happened. As the mother Brachiosaurus stopped to graze in the forest, Alex and Cathy slid down her body to the ground.

After what they had just lived through, it was clear to Alex that this was a world in which the strongest survive. He and Cathy certainly did not have the size or strength to be included in that category.

"We have to get out of here NOW. I don't know where we are going to go, but, just not here."

"Wait a minute before we go", Cathy shouted as she took off running towards the mother Brachiosaurus. Upon finding her in the herd, Cathy wrapped her small arms as far around the dinosaur's tree stump sized leg as she could reach and squeezed tightly. "Good-bye, thank you." As if the Brachiosaurus understood, she lowered her head, nibbled Cathy's head in a kind of "good-bye" kiss.

Cathy skipped back to where Alex and the juvenile Brachiosaurus were waiting. They both hugged the lovable creature and kissed him on both sides of his face. The three of them stood there. He was supposed to leave them, but he did not understand. When he wouldn't leave, they both got behind him to push him towards his mother figuring he would get that hint. They did not want him to follow them wherever they were liable to go.

At last, the juvenile realized what Alex and Cathy were trying to "tell" him. Off he trotted towards the herd craning his head over his shoulder as he lumbered along.

"Let's go over to the clearing so we will be in open space", Alex told Cathy. "Maybe the compass will find North this time. We'll see if it can lead us home."

Once, in the clearing, Alex removed the compass from his pocket. He held it in the flat of his hand closing his eyes wishing for it to take them home.

Immediately the compass needle began rotating, repeating its earlier actions. It began spinning rapidly as if the dial would fly off the base. When it stopped, everything around them went out of control. Both Alex and Cathy were knocked to the ground from the mere force of the wind being generated by the swirling world. Everything was completely blurred. They squeezed their eyes shut against the visual motion and the dust that was being kicked up all around them.

Abruptly, all was still. They gasped for air as they opened their eyes to see the world into which they had been thrown. This world looked very much like their own – similar trees, flowering plants, grasses, annoying insects buzzing around them, and the now familiar wings of the large black bird soaring directly towards the sun. "Are we home Alex?"

As Alex surveyed their new environment, he spotted a troop of Utahraptors rapidly approaching. "No, we are definitely not home", Alex exclaimed. These creatures looked more than menacing. They were nineteen feet tall with large piercing eyes, pointed fangs that spelled danger, long hands with sharp claws, and a huge curved claw on their second toe. Obviously, they were on a hunt. Alex did not want to be their dinner.

They were fortunate to be standing near a tall broad leaf tree with very low hanging thick branches. "Start climbing the tree and keep going as high as you can", Alex told his sister as he gave her a boost up to reach the first branch. He didn't waste any time looking around. Alex jumped onto the branch and did not look back.

They climbed higher and higher. It was none too soon. As they settled themselves in a fork of upper branches, they looked down. They saw three Utahraptors pacing the clearing in a circle around the tree, looking up. Every once in a while, one of them would bare his teeth while leaping at the tree trunk. He would dig his sharp claws into the bark to try to get a hold on the trunk so he could climb up to get them. He wasn't able to get a hook into the trunk so would slide down scraping his claws into the bark as he descended. The noise, like chalk screeching on a blackboard, was excruciating.

This seemed to be a "stand-off" game which the Utahraptors seemed to understand. Alex and Cathy were stuck in the tree while the Utahraptors were blocking their only escape route as they waited patiently for their taste of human flesh.

Suddenly, the Utahraptor with the brightest head plume spun around. He ran off into the trees leaving the other two to guard their "dinner". What sounded like a scuffle was going on in the brush hidden by the trees. A loud moan became a muffled sound. After only a moment of complete silence, a roar of triumph was heard. The other two Utahraptors responded to this cry by running off in the direction of the sound. The Utahraptor was dragging his bloody kill towards the clearing. Soon all three were feasting on the carcass.

The sight of them feeding was nauseating but, at least, Alex and Cathy apparently had been forgotten. Quietly, Alex motioned to Cathy to follow him. They were going to make their escape down the tree. When they got to the lower branches, they saw that while one of the Utahraptors was still eating, actually crushing bones with his teeth, another was laying down, and the third had wandered off.

It was risky to get out of the tree without knowing where the third Utahraptor had gone, but Alex felt they had no choice.

"Cathy this is our chance. Now or never." Alex whispered. "I'll go down first. If they don't move, follow me – fast and quiet. If they do come after me, climb back up the tree, close your eyes, and wait."

"You can't leave me alone."

"Just listen, for once in your life. Don't talk back to me!" he screamed at her in a hushed whisper. Cathy was annoying him while he was trying to concentrate. Once again, he was sounding like his mother. Now he was beginning to understand why his mother said what she always said. But this was not the time to be thinking of that. He was terrified for their lives. He had to concentrate on getting them away, safely.

Alex made it to the ground. One Utahraptor looked over, but continued to feast on the cracked bones. Alex raised his arms to help Cathy down. Once down, they scurried into the underbrush just like the small mammals that lived there.

The branches were alive, withering about their bodies like snakes. The thorns were scratching and tearing at their clothes and skin. When they finally crawled through the underbrush, they found themselves in a wide clearing the size of a football field.

There, in the center of the clearing was a herd of humongous creatures with enormous neck frills, two horns above their eyes and a smaller one on their snouts. These could only be Torosaurus. At least they were herbivores. Alex could not get over their size. The frill alone was at least three times Cathy's height. The children had to be careful. They were like pebbles among gigantic boulders.

Off to the side of the clearing apparently watching over the herd was one Torosaurus larger than all the rest. He must have been at least thirty feet long and probably weighed 6 tons. He was the dominate bull - the Alpha of the herd. Most of the others were gathered in a small area to his left, causally ingesting anything and everything green. The remaining few animals were standing alone off to his right. These animals were staring directly at the alpha male yet, also seemed to be on guard. Alex felt a stillness in the air. Although all appeared to be tranquil, there was a tension floating among these animals. Cathy and he stayed huddled at the edge of the clearing – watching, waiting.

Gradually one of the lone Torosaurus started to amble over to where the large bull was standing. His gait continuously increased until he was at a full run, head lowered, and horns ready to gore the alpha male. This looked to be the beginning foray of a battle for dominance of the herd.

The crashing sound when their horns locked sounded like two huge garbage trucks colliding head on. Massive pressure was exerted by each male by striking their heads against each other. The younger Torosaurus seemed intent on inflicting mortal wounds to the alpha male. The older more experienced Torosaurus was merely deflecting the blows using his massive bulk to push his opponent away. The battle created a tornado of dust partially hiding both of the Torosaurus. The grunts and cries were echoing throughout the entire forest.

With the dust settling to the ground, Alex saw the younger Torosaurus limping away painfully. One of his large horns had broken near the base during the conflict and was dangling down his face. Without the full use of his horns, he would never be able to challenge a dominate male again. Since the horns were also used for protection, his future survival would be questionable. The dominate bull raised his head high letting out a roar of triumph for all to hear. He was still the Alpha Male of the herd.

The alpha male moved slowly toward the small creek running through the center of the clearing. It did not matter that an Ankylosaurus was already on the bank of the creek drinking his fill. The two herbivores lived in a peaceful relationship with each other. They had a common enemy – the carnivores.

Alex and Cathy were also thirsty. They went to the creek at the opposite end of the clearing. Alex kept a watchful eye as Cathy drank the crystal clear cool water and then she did the same for him. While they were drinking, the Ankylosaurus slowly ambled towards them. He was built like the armored tank in Alex's set of military toys. His entire body was covered with large, bony plates. The end of his tail was frightening. It was a large bony club which he used as a defensive weapon against the predators. The Ankylosaurus lifted his head and sniffed the air. They had a highly developed sense of smell.

"What do we do now?" Cathy asked nervously.

"Try to be calm. No sudden motions."

They slowly got to their feet. Cathy followed Alex as he stepped into the shallow creek and waded across to the other bank. The Ankylosaurus turned his head, watching them. Suddenly he leaped, as well as a tank could leap, into the creek. He came up on the other side placing himself between them and the brush surrounding the clearing; thus blocking any escape that Alex may have been contemplating.

While Alex was trying to figure out their next move, they heard a rustling sound from the direction of the bushes. Out of the brush a small dinosaur emerged, flashing its teeth, and growling like an angry dog. He tried running around the six-and-a-half-ton tank to get at Alex and Cathy but the giant Ankylosaurus kept blocking his way. At one point the Ankylosaurus head-butted the ferocious creature, knocking him to the ground. The small dinosaur let out a yelp.

"I think he is a baby. He's cute with his feathery head and little tail" Cathy thought that anything young was "cute". Not in this world!

"Cathy, he's not so cute. Look at those teeth he keeps snapping with. He could take a real big bite out of us with no problem. We have to be careful", Alex said as he began backing up into the creek again. Cathy decided not to take any chances. She closely followed him into the water.

The commotion and the strange aroma in the air coming from the other end of the creek piqued the curiosity of some of the Torosaurus. They came over to investigate both the strange smelling creatures that were in their midst and the small violent dinosaur who was crying out. The Torosaurus surrounded him. They began to push him around as if he were a ball. With each shove his cries got steadier, louder, and more desperate.

All play ended abruptly when an earth-shattering roar was heard. The leaves began to shimmy from the sound vibrations. The trees shook as the branches parted to reveal the most dreaded monster of the entire dinosaur era. An extremely angry forty-foot-tall Tyrannosaurus Rex emerged. She quickly went on the offensive attacking the Torosaurus who were surrounding the small dinosaur. Once she scattered them, she looked directly into the creek and focused her attention on Alex and Cathy. They ran out of the creek to the other side.

With one step, the Tyrannosaurus Rex was over the creek after them. Cathy started screaming. Alex began looking for an escape. He could not see any way out so he just hugged Cathy tightly, "We'll be ok. You'll see." His only solution was to pull her into a grove of trees hoping the trees would deter the furious dinosaur.

When Alex turned around to see where she was, he saw the Ankylosaurus step towards the angry Tyrannosaurus Rex. His tail was raised and a sharp blow was delivered to the Tyrannosaurus Rex's back. The blow inflicted searing pain. She spun around going after the Ankylosaurus. Even with her long sharp serrated teeth it was hard to crack the armor of the Ankylosaurus unless she bit him in the right spot. She clawed and bit at him while he kept pounding her with his massive tail club every chance he got. The bloody battle continued with the Ankylosaurus working his way gradually back toward the creek and the young, bellowing Tyrannosaurus Rex.

With the child being threatened, the Tyrannosaurus Rex abandoned the fight. The Ankylosaurus stood firm as the Tyrannosaurus Rex rushed back to the young dinosaur to comfort him in his distress. After checking to make sure nothing other than his childish pride was wounded, she ushered him back into the trees. They disappeared into the oncoming twilight. The fight would probably continue another day.

The herd of Torosaurus seemed to be settling down for the night. Their hero, the Ankylosaurus collapsed at the edge of the creek guarding against an abrupt return of the Tyrannosaurus Rex.

Alex and Cathy were wet, and hungry, yet, too exhausted to even think about anything except, sleep. They curled up against each other in the grove of trees where they had hidden from the Tyrannosaurus Rex. By the time the stars began to twinkle, they were sound asleep.

The new day dawned unlike any other Alex and Cathy had experienced in this strange world. There was an unprecedented silence – no wind through the leaves, no sound of small mammals scampering through the brush, no thunderous sounds of the dinosaurs as they moved about grazing or hunting. There was complete quiet.

Cathy, too, noticed the change, "Why is there no noise?"

"I'm not sure. First things first. I'm hungry and I'm sure you are too. Let's find something to eat", Alex said as he moved down the path checking leaves as he went looking for signs that the Torosaurus had been eating them. That would indicate that it probably would be safe for them to eat them also. For the first time in their lives, they would be eating their vegetables. Their Mom would be pleased.

"May I help you?" asked the elderly white-haired lady at the School Group Check-In desk.

"I hope so. I think we lost two of our campers", answered Shanisha, her voice trembling nervously.

"Don't worry. Children wander off all the time. We haven't LOST one in all my years here. I'll get George to help you look for them."

As she was speaking, the sympathetic lady made a phone call. "Hola Jorge, necesitamos tu ayuda. Al parecer dos niños se han desaparecido en uno de los grupos."

Within a few minutes, a tall uniformed guard arrived at the desk. "¿Que está pasando Señora Gomez?"

Ms. Gomez answered him in English so Shanisha would understand the conversation, "a deuce on the loose," she responded with a laugh.

It was no laughing matter to Shanisha. A tall, bald 40 something year old man approached her. Since he was wearing a uniform, Shanisha assumed he must be George. "Where did you last see the children?" She told him it was in the Hall of African Mammals. "Well, let's go. That will be our starting point", George said in a reassuring voice.

Up the stairs they went – straight to the Hall of African Mammals. They searched the Hall thoroughly, but there was no sign of Alex or Cathy.

At the far end of the hall standing in the doorway, they saw another guard. George went over to him. "Tom, did you see a little boy and girl wandering around by themselves this morning?"

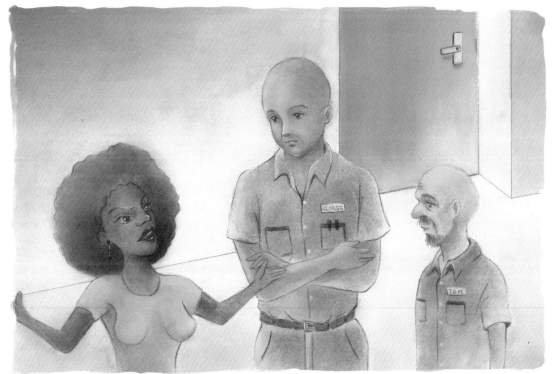

"Yes, they asked where to find the dinosaurs. They said they were meeting their mother at the exhibit. I thought it was strange, but, you know, modern parents can be strange. I sent them to the fourth floor."

Now, they had a definite clue as to where to search. Shanisha and George headed up to the Dinosaur Exhibit.

They searched the floor from one end to the other, but there was no sign of Alex and Cathy. The last gallery to investigate was the room of the Saurischian Dinosaurs which included the feared Tyrannosaurus Rex.

As Shanisha walked down the aisle created by the rows of display cases, she saw a long, slender object shimmering on the floor at the base of one of the cases. She was drawn directly to the object. It was a long, black feather so dark it reflected the light.

"This is strange," exclaimed Shanisha as she picked up the feather. Once in her hand, she felt a cold shiver go down her spine. She had an empty feeling in her stomach. She felt the ghostly presence of Alex and Cathy. But she did not see them. She saw no one other than George.

"How did this get inside the Dinosaur Hall?" she wondered.

"Where are they?" she asked herself.

Frustrated at not finding the children, George told Shanisha that she should join the rest of her group while he organized a team of security guards to conduct a full search of the museum.

Reluctantly, Shanisha agreed. She walked down the stairs to join the group who, by then, had arrived at the movie theater for their scheduled show. She left George and the museum authorities to conduct the search.

She found Todd in the theater and sat down, with a sigh, in the seat he had saved for her. She told him all that had happened or, rather, all that did not happen upstairs. No counselors had ever "lost" a camper. They were both very nervous. They settled into their seats – hoping for the best.

Endless days seemed to pass. The stillness and silence continued. Their time was consumed with finding food - leaves and roots they had seen the dinosaurs eat - avoiding dinosaurs, and securing a safe place to sleep.

One day while they were foraging, they heard low grumble sounds developing which intensified in volume and ferocity until it became a deafening sound hurting their ear drums.

"Alex!" Cathy cried out.

"I don't know! I don't know! Come with me." In frustration and survival mode, Alex grabbed Cathy's hand. They ran to the base of a large boulder to huddle in the safety of the overhanging rock. Just as they reached the boulder, the entire mountain seemed to vibrate. Small rocks were rolling around and being tossed into the air. The roar increased, if that was possible.

Mammals were scurrying for cover; dinosaurs seemed to be stampeding away from the direction of the mountain, and the air was filled with flying reptiles.

Cathy and Alex stayed close to the shelter of the rock, hugging each other as much for comfort as for protection against whatever was to come. They stayed in the same position all afternoon and throughout the long night.

When dawn broke, the world seemed to be calm, but there was a difference. There was a sour acidic smell in the air. Their nostrils burned as they breathed the poisoned air. The sky, instead of being clear, bright blue with hints of gold like it usually is at dawn, was obscured with a massive cloud of blackened, reddish dust. The air was heavy. Cathy was having difficulty breathing.

"Hold on; take deep breaths. Stay calm." This has happened before so Cathy knew what she needed to do. Alex grabbed Cathy's backpack and started rummaging through it to find her asthma inhaler. Finally, there it was in the side zip pocket. "You can always count on Mom", thought Alex.

"Here, use your inhaler and we'll figure this one out."

Just when Cathy settled into a normal breathing pattern, a deafening explosion was heard. Before they could DO anything, they were being showered by small fiery rocks and buckets of black ash.

A pebble hit Cathy's arm. She screamed, more in shock than pain as the hot pebble burnt her flesh.

As she turned towards Alex for protection, a gigantic Ornithocheirus with an enormous wing span swooped out of the red ochre clouds grabbing Cathy with one of its talons. Before it could lift higher into the sky, Alex wrapped his arms around the other leg. Both of them were being lifted high into the sky.

Alex managed to scramble his way up the Ornithocheirus' leg to climb onto his sturdy back. He leaned down the side of the body reaching for Cathy. "Take my arm. I'll pull you up." Although she was frightened beyond belief, Alex's voice was reassuring. She took his arm with both hands. The moment she did, the Ornithocheirus released his hold on her which allowed Alex to pull her up to the creature's firm wing. He pulled her along the wing so she was with him on the Ornithocheirus' back.

With Alex and Cathy firmly planted, the Ornithocheirus started flying higher and higher in a zig-zag, random pattern to avoid the flaming pebbles. Higher and higher they went with the Ornithocheirus. Alex winced in pain every time a burning pebble stuck him. At last, they were above the red haze flying still higher in a swirling pattern into a clear blue atmosphere towards a shimmering light.

Abruptly the Pterosaur reversed course. They were in a rapidly increasing nosedive straight to the ground. Alex and Cathy tightly embraced the Ornithocheirus' neck just to keep from sliding off. Total darkness descended upon them.

Suddenly everything was still. Light exploded like a blinding bolt of lightning. The lights in the room flickered, then gradually became constant and bright. Alex saw that they were in a large room with assorted types of Pterosaurs including the Ornithocheirus soaring on a large movie screen.

Cathy was beside him. All the kids, Todd and Shanisha were in the seats around him. It appeared that they were safe, back in their world, back in the Museum of Natural History. Alex passed out.

"Wake up Alex. Wake up. It's almost time to go. We don't want to be late." Cathy was screaming at him while excitedly jumping around the room. Alex opened his eyes. He was in his bedroom with Cathy using a large glimmering black feather to tickle him awake. "Get that away from me! I'm awake." He was awake but completely confused. He looked at Cathy. She appeared normal. Then he noticed a small burn mark on her arm. "Where did that come from?"

"I don't know. I just woke up with it. It doesn't hurt though", she replied. Since he was up, Cathy skipped out of the room to brush her teeth. Alex slowly got out of bed.

On the floor, at the foot of the bed, was his orange Day Camp T shirt covered with a thick layer of reddish, black soot. Alex looked around his familiar room. He gasped when he saw a large black silhouette of a bird covering the framed family photographs which were hung on the far wall. Alex spun his head to the window to see what was casting the shadow. On the windowsill was a coal black bird. He stared, in shock, directly into the depths of the bird's dark eyes. The bird stared back, intensely. This direct connection seemed to last for a long time. The trance was finally broken when the bird lowered her head as if in a nod to say, "Good-bye". She turned and immediately spread her wings to take off directly into the sun.

As Alex was trying to figure out what had been happening, he heard a loud crash – the shattering of glass. He turned towards the thunderous sound. At first, he only saw a rainbow of light as the shards of glass glistened in the sunlight creating a prism of color. Then he realized that the photograph of Uncle Stefan teaching him how to use the compass had fallen to the floor.

Was there some symbolism in the glass shattering? Did it mean they were finally released from the glass?

Quickly, Alex picked his cargo shorts off the floor. He reached into the front pocket feeling the familiar round shape of his compass. He took it out. Placing the compass in the palm of his hand, the arrow initially showed some hesitation then, fast movement which abruptly stopped. The arrow pointed towards N for North. He was in his world!

Whether it would be reality or fantasy, Alex knew that he was ready for today's adventure.

GLOSSARY OF DINOSAURS
(in order of appearance)

BAROSAURUS – The name means "heavy lizard". This was a giant herbivore about 89 feet long with 4/5^{ths} of his total length being his neck and tail of the late Jurassic period (about 150 million years ago).

SAURISCHIAN – A category of lizard hipped dinosaurs: 1.) theropods (carnivores – meat eaters) such as Allosaurus and Tyrannosaurus Rex and 2.) sauropods (herbivores – plant eaters) such as the Brachiosaurus.

DEINONYCHUS – Refers to the hooked claw found on the hind feet, the Deinonychus, "terrible claw" was about 11 feet long and weighed about 170 pounds. Scientific studies have led to the theory that birds are descended from these dinosaurs.

PLATEOSAURUS – The "broad lizard" was from the late Triassic Period (216 -200 million years ago). They were a bipedal (walking on two legs) herbivore with a small skull and long flexible neck. The adults were between 16 and 33 feet long weighing between 1300 and 8800 pounds.

LILIENSTERNUS – These were moderate size (17 feet long, 280 pounds) bipedal ground dwelling carnivores of the later part of the Triassic Period (about 210 million years ago).

BRACHIOSAURUS – Giant herbivores of the genus Saurischian about 85 feet long and weighing between 3 and 45 tons. These dinosaurs had a long neck, small head and a relatively short tail. They are thought to have consumed between 440 and 880 pounds of plants each day.

ALLOSAURUS – Their name means "different lizard". These bipedal carnivores of the late Jurassic Period of the genus Saurischian had large heads which were counter balanced by a long heavy tail. They were 28 feet tall and weighed about 2.3 tons with large sharp teeth and short arms with sharp curved claws on each of the three fingers per arm.

UTAHRAPTORS – Since the first specimens were found in Utah, these dinosaurs were named Utahraptors meaning "Utah's predator". They were carnivores from the early Cretaceous Period. Estimated to be 23 feet long, about 1100 pounds, these bipedal hunters had large curved claws on their 2nd toes.

TOROSAURUS – Named for large openings on its frill, the Torosaurus, "perforated lizard" lived during the Cretaceous Period (68 million years ago). The frilled skull reached up to 9 feet in length. The Torosaurus was between 25 and 30 feet long and weighed 4 to 6 tons.

ANKYLOSAURUS –The Ankylosaurus was covered with body armor – huge plates of bone embedded into the skin to protect against attackers. They also possessed a massive tail club which when welded in defending itself could break the bones of another dinosaur. This giant herbivore lived at the end of the Cretaceous Period (about 66 million years ago). He was 30 feet in length and weighed about 13,000 pounds (6.5 tons).

TYRANNOSAURUS REX – The name itself "tyrant lizard king" is enough to bring a sense of terror. They were 42 feet in length and could weigh up to 7 tons. They were bipedal with long, heavy tails possessing small arms with two clawed fingers. These ferocious carnivores of the genus Saurischian lived in the late Cretaceous Period.

ORNITHOCHEIRUS – These flying reptiles of the Pterosaur genus who were 10 feet long with a wing span of 20 feet weighing between 50 and 100 pounds were from the Cretaceous Period (100 million years ago). It has been assumed that their main diet was fish. They are unique in that they had a crest on both the top and bottom of their beak which may have been used to crack open crustacean shells.

Acknowledgments

It seems like I have always had ideas for stories geared for children, yet actually writing a book proved to be far more daunting than I could ever have imagined. *Beyond the Swirl* would have remained merely a draft of a story had it not been for the encouragement and support of my best friend, Vladimir Rios. From reading draft after draft, making structural and character suggestions to collaborating with Chi Fung Wong, the illustrator, and myself to insure the illustrations conveyed the mood and feeling of the story, Rios has ridden the creative roller coaster along with me. He continuously encouraged me to strive for excellence. I owe him a special thanks of gratitude for everything he has done to make this book a reality.

I am forever indebted to my exceptional artist, Chi Fung Wong, for visually capturing the characters and storyline of the book. His work has brought the story to life.

Creating and writing a book is a surreal process. Thankfully, I had the grounding editorial help and knowledge of my sister, Elaine Ann Blum, to review the drafts, make story suggestions, and correct my grammar. In all my endeavors, she has always been there to lend her love and support. Thank you!

During the process, friends were recruited to read the book to offer suggestions. Gerard Woods was one such individual who tackled the role with sincerity and seriousness. His keen insight which lead to many editorial improvements was highly appreciated.

While the dinosaurs were researched extensively prior to putting pen to paper, evidence is constantly being unearthed which dispels some of the previously held truths. Marion Schultheis, who has extensive knowledge of dinosaurs, reviewed both the content and illustrations to confirm current accuracy. I am grateful to Marion for her work on *Beyond the Swirl*.

CPSIA information can be obtained at www.ICGtesting.com
Printed in the USA
BVIW121339180819
555916BV00007B/1